LEVEL 1 READER

BOB BOOKS®

W9-DIV-775

My School Trip

by LYNN MASLEN KERTELL
illustrated by SUE HENDRA

SCHOLASTIC INC.

Jack's class is going on a trip.

They will take a bus to the zoo.

Jack sits with Bill.

The zoo is full of things to see.
Jack hears the chatter of animal
sounds.

Bill sniffs new smells.

Jack and Bill see zebras and giraffes.

Next, Jack and Bill see goats.

Jack hears, "Ruh, ruh, roarrrrrr!"
What makes that sound?

That sound came from a tiger.

Jack hears the tiger roar another loud roar.

Next, the class sees polar bears.

Bill hears a new sound. "*Hoot, hoot, hoot.*"
It is not an owl. What can it be?

"Monkeys!" yells Bill.
"I can't hear you," shouts Jack.

The monkeys hoot, howl, and yelp.
They are very loud.

Hoot!

Bill wants to follow his nose.

But Jack can hear screeching around the corner.

Screech, Screech!

Little birds make big, screeching noises!

Jack can feed the birds.

Jack's class sits down for lunch.
They listen to the sounds of the zoo.

They hear a shout. *Hello! Hello!*
A peacock yells its greeting from the
roof.

The peacock wants lunch.
A man from the zoo feeds the bird.

Jack and Bill find a gift from the peacock.

The kids hear another sound.
"*Ha, ha, ha!*" What makes that sound?

Is it a frog? Is it a wild dog?
Is it a bird?

It is children yelling!

Jack's class joins in and makes the sounds of the zoo.

They roar, hoot, screech, and yell!

Whee!